FIRST

DARK AGES

Future Chron Universe

Volume 23

To The Stars Series

Book 2

D.W. PATTERSON

Tenth Printing – May, 2023

1

The Kress family had come to the nearest tower complex from their farm which provided many foodstuffs to the complex. Once every quarter Stanley Kress would make the trip to meet with his customers, the food conglomerates; to address current supply problems, future needs, and sometimes slow payment. The farm was completely automated and business as usual continued while the family was away.

The tower complexes were like old Earth cities but much more compact. There were no suburbs or exurbs surrounding the complexes. They were a huge agglomeration of humanity and technology. With millions of residents, each complex was an overwhelming challenge to manage efficiently. So far only artificial intelligence had been successful at such management. But those years were over and human government was finding difficulty in replacing them.

"Okay," said Stanley Kress to his wife Betty. "I'm going down to the corporate offices to see what has happened with the orders."

"And our payments," said his wife.

"Of course honey."

"I'm going to take the kids to the museum. You want to meet us at Drago's for a late lunch?"

"Sure honey, about two?" he said as he kissed her.

"Right," she said.

Drago's was across from Westside City Park. Betty and the kids had finished the museum a bit early and were enjoying the park. She had sent a message to Stanley that they were waiting for him there.

She was watching the kids play when just beyond she saw a crowd gathering. Soon it became clear to her that what at first had seemed like happenstance was obviously a planned gathering, maybe organically organized. Many in the crowd were carrying signs and a few were erecting a mobile platform. Before long a couple of loudspeakers had been installed and someone was approaching the platform.

Once the person had mounted the platform he began speaking. Betty could easily hear him.

"Fellow citizens. We are here to protest! The government wants us to be docile and follow orders but we are here to protest! Orders they say, orders that will lead to our death, I say! It is, and has always been our right to protest! To protest the government's inept handling of this crisis. Ever since they dismissed the AIs from the complex we have been at risk of privation, starvation and worse.

"It is our right not to starve, it is our right not to wait until we are dying from hunger, not to wait until we can't protest! It is our right to tell the government that we want a change! A change for the better! And if they can't do it we will do it ourselves!"

The crowd had been following his every word and exploded into applause and cheering.

Just before the speaker could begin again the sound of sirens could be heard approaching. Before long the crowd could be seen falling back as if being herded. Butterfly bombs appeared above them. The weapons were small insect shaped flying canisters that dipped and dove like a butterfly to avoid any defense against them. Once reaching the desired location they showered the area with a mild nano-agent that caused the victim to lose control of leg and arm muscles. The agent was targeted to deliver only to those muscle groups and the effect would wear off within a few minutes.

The herd of people was now running directly toward Betty and her children with the butterflies following. Betty became alarmed as it appeared that the crowd would make it to them. She jumped up and ran toward her children yelling for them to come to her. The kids were confused, one started crying. Almost to her children, Betty became overwhelmed with the rushing crowd and before she could turn she heard the noise above her, a butterfly bomb had dropped its load. Betty went down with the rest of the people in her area falling across another woman. She heard bones cracking. And there they both lay, neither able to move as the police closed in.

Stanley was a little late. Standing in front of Drago's he looked across the street to the park where he was supposed to meet Betty and the kids. He could see police drones above the play area and people rushing to leave this side of the park. Something was happening.

Stanley rushed across the street without bothering to use the crosswalk. Arriving in the park he ran to the area set aside for the children's play equipment. The area was almost empty now. Seeing a policeman a few yards beyond he called out.

"I'm looking for my wife and children!"

The policeman began walking toward him. Stanley moved to meet the man. As he was coming up to the officer, Stanley was about to ask about his family again when the cop held his arm out and sprayed something in his face. Stanley went down but not out. He was looking from face to face without comprehension of what had happened as the officers carried him from the field and into one of their vehicles. They roughly tossed him in back. He felt other arms grasp him and drag him across the floor. Then he passed out.

Stanley awoke in a darkened room. It seemed to be late in the night. His head hurt but his arms seemed to be working again because he automatically rubbed his aching skull. Eventually, he sat up and looked around. He seemed to be in a good-sized room with many others. At first, he thought that maybe his wife and children would be in there with him. But he eventually realized that only adult males shared the room with him.

Stanley wondered what time it was but found that his AI assistant had been taken from him. He had no way of knowing how long he sat there, maybe an hour, maybe more when a guard came to the barred door window and called out his name. Stanley, who hadn't noticed the window, got up, shaking a bit, and answered. The guard motioned for him to come to the door.

Standing in front of the door Stanley noticed the barred window had disappeared and then the door recessed into the wall. The guard warned him to not make any sudden moves or he would spray him again. He was taken to a small room with a table and seated on one side by the guard who then retired.

The virtual avatars appeared and began talking.

"You are Stanley Kress?" said the male avatar.

"That is correct."

"And you reside at 1487 National Highway, Atkinson Territory?" said the female avatar.

"Yes."

"You are a farmer?"

"Yes."

"You have a wife, Betty and two children, Stanley Jr. and Concey?"

"Yes, that is correct. Can you tell me about them? I went to the . . ."

The female avatar held up her hand.

"Just a minute Mr. Kress, we will get to that in a minute."

The avatars kept questioning him. Useless questions about his politics, the agrarian union he belonged to, the farm's finances.

After almost an hour the female said, "Okay, I think we have enough Mr. Kress. If you would wait here we will send in your wife."

And just like that Betty appeared as the door recessed. Stanley noticed that her arm was in a medical sleeve usually used to protect a bone that had been broken and rapid-healed.

He ran to her. They embraced, Betty cried.

"Oh Stanley these people won't tell me anything about the children."

"It's okay dear. Now that we are together the next step is to find out where the children are and what has happened."

"But they won't tell me honey."

"They will dear when I get our lawyer involved."

But the lawyer was unable to find out anything. The best he could do was plead Stanley and Betty guilty of participating in a public disturbance and getting them off with a year's probation and the requirement that they not leave Atkinson Territory for the next year.

Stanley was outraged, but yelling at his lawyer solved nothing. He and Betty would have to leave the complex. After a month of legalities and hearings, they would go home empty-handed. Stanley would put a detective on the case but the detective found no leads. At the last meeting in the detective's office, he whispered to Stanley that he believed the case was being covered up at the highest levels of government. Stanley wondered why the detective was whispering in his own office.

Betty was devastated and all but quit trying to help her husband with the farm. Despite the automation, the farm declined as Stanley didn't much care either.

2

The Aggies (Artificial General Intelligence) had controlled the Earth's fortunes for some three centuries before they had become involved in a civil war with a breakaway faction of Aggies. The resulting war had not only destroyed AIs and their infrastructure but also their human charges, both virtual and real-world.

People enraged with the resulting loss of lives demanded their government's do something. The governments decided to make an example of the Earth's AIs. They canceled their management contracts and demanded the Aggies vacate their government-provided installations.

The Aggies used their substantial resources to flee into space aboard fourth-generation fusion ships with the new wormhole drive. They intended to reestablish themselves either somewhere else in the Solar System or exosolar. They were determined to no longer be dependent on humans in any manner. They headed for Titan which was an independent Republic and known for its openness to technical expertise.

With the Aggies gone the tower complexes on Earth were left without effective governance. Now that the human governments were in charge they were slow in getting organized and were somewhat at a loss as to how to manage the complexes, since the Aggies had handled them for so long.

And the people of the hundred or so tower complexes who made up nearly ninety percent of the Earth's population were becoming concerned. Food shortages were becoming common, utilities were becoming unreliable and the residents, who had never had to deal with such situations in their lives, panicked.

"We've got to take matters into our own hands," said Joe Carthy. "The government isn't going to do anything for us. They can't take care of a hundred complexes, I doubt they can take care of one."

The crowd that had gathered around Carthy began to stir.

What if he's right? What can we do?

Carthy sensing they were turning his way continued.

"What should we do?" he asked and waited, turning from face to face.

"First we secure our food and water supply. Without those, we aren't going to survive.

"How do we do that?

"I say we take it. Each store. One by one. Until every store in this complex is under our control. With the food supply secure we then storm the waterworks. Until this crisis is over we make those resources free to every citizen that joins us. And those that don't? Well they'll have to decide for themselves whether they can survive without us."

Just then a police car rolled up. Two policemen made their way through the crowd of about one hundred and called for Carthy to get down from his perch on the low wall surrounding the city fountain. Carthy called them fascists and warned them their time was coming.

The police officers seized Carthy and dragged him off the wall. Before he knew it he had a knee in his back and his arms restrained behind him. Carthy yelled to the crowd to help but before anyone stepped forward one of the officers applied a stun pod to the side of his head. Carthy was quiet and docile now. The officers quickly led him to the police car, placed him inside, and were away. The crowd milled about for a minute and then dispersed as police drones watched overhead.

The fourth public disturbance of the day had been quelled but it was just the beginning.

It had been a month since the Aggies had left Earth. Patrice Williams was watching the disturbances on her wallscreen along with her best friend Agnes Jefferson.

Without turning from the screen Agnes said, "No lemons today."

"What's that Agnes?"

"You know how I couldn't place my grocery order online and I said I'd have to go to the store in person?"

"Yeah I remember."

"Well I went to the store this morning and got a few things but they were out of most of what I wanted including lemons. You know how I like fresh lemons."

"Yeah I know. What did the store say?"

"The produce man said he didn't know when they would get in another batch. Something wrong with the supply chain or something."

"I've never heard of such a thing in my life," said Patrice.

"Lot's of things we've never heard of in our lives, just look at the screen," said Agnes.

The demonstration on the screen had attracted thousands of people. The police were out in the hundreds. The whole of the sector was disrupted. No one had ever seen anything like it.

Suddenly at the very corner of the screen, a scuffle broke out between members of the crowd and the police. Police clubs could be seen hammering up and down. Ten, twenty clubs in unison like some choreographed play. The protesters began to give, the police moved as a solid curtain always with the clubs rising and falling. Behind the line of advancing police a few of the crowd were down receiving a final kick from an officer before he moved on.

Patrice and Agnes were horrified. Unable to comprehend what they were seeing and unable to turn away. It was as if the world as they knew it no longer existed and some kind of strange substitute had taken its place.

The food riots had begun.

As the days passed and conditions deteriorated Patrice and Agnes decided to share Patrice's apartment on the second floor as a way of feeling safer. Agnes had lost her job because of the general downturn in the economy and after being trapped in the elevator on her way to her own tenth-floor apartment had decided the second floor was more convenient. Not being on the ground floor it provided the women with a sense of safety while at the same time it would allow them to evacuate by the stairs quickly if needed.

Agnes was cooking a little afternoon meal when Patrice got home from her job.

"Hi Patrice how's it going?"

"Agnes it's getting awful out there. Here's the wine," she said as she entered the small kitchen.

"It's probably the last bottle I'll be able to afford. The cost is skyrocketing. Up fifty percent since last week."

"I agree Patrice, we should only spend our money on staples until this craziness is over."

"I'll be back after I change," said Patrice heading for her bedroom.

The table set and the wine poured, the two women sat down to eat with the wallscreen on but muted.

"I finally got the food credits," said Agnes.

"Oh that's good," said Patrice.

"Yeah, I was in that office for four hours today starting at eight this morning. I think they only approved me because I've lived there for the past week."

"I don't understand? You couldn't do this online?"

"No, I never got through. It seems the networks are almost useless since the Aggies left. It's like we're living in the dark ages."

"Still the credits, they will be helpful. Uh-oh," said Patrice looking at the wallscreen.

Agnes turned to see.

On the screen, the women saw a military unit using butterfly bombs against an unruly crowd at Westside City Park.

As the butterflies delivered their loads the sight was like seeing a wave of staggering, falling people spreading concentrically from the drop zone. From the distance of the camera, it seemed as if dominoes were falling. The bodies prone but the heads turning from side to side as the victims tried to see what was happening around them. Even the area around the children's playground was engulfed in the chaos. It was disconcerting to the women. They continued to stare at the wallscreen even as it cut to a reporter whom they couldn't hear.

"How did this happen?" asked Patrice.

"You mean the riot we just saw?"

"No, I mean how did we get here, to this place?"

"Well some people think it was because the government dismissed the Aggies without preparation."

"Well of course," said Patrice, "but I thought we were beyond this level of fear and hatred. I thought the system would continue, maybe with some small disruptions but nothing like what we are seeing."

"I was talking to a gentleman just this morning about that. He seemed to think that in many ways we have regressed over time. And he didn't mean in our capabilities to fend for ourselves. We haven't been able to do that in hundreds of years. We're so interdependent now.

"Anyway, what he meant is that the people left here on Earth have self-selected for dependency. Those with more ambition and drive have all left for solar and extra-solar destinations. And others have entered the meta-verse."

"Oh the meta-verse, it's so horrible what is happening. I heard today that they lost another computing center, millions of metizens probably terminated."

"It is horrible, isn't it? But getting back to what I was saying. If what this man says is true we are in for much worse than we've seen so far. Without the Aggies to stop the slide we could soon be unable to live in these huge complexes. We simply don't have the necessary skills to keep them up."

"If he's right, how long does he think we have?"

"At the most months, maybe just weeks."

"It's not fair," said Davy Jackson. "Why do we have to suffer for the idiocy of the previous generations?" Davy and his friends made up a group in their early teens that had opposed Aggie control and now found the new situation just as unacceptable. They were looking for a way out. Unlike many their age they had no interest in the meta-verse and now after the recent disasters that didn't seem like a choice anymore. There were only two other members of the group with Davy at the time.

"We've got to get off this planet," said Jimy.

"We're underage, we couldn't get a rocket to anywhere without our parent's permission," said Linda whom the others called Lind.

"I've got an idea," said Davy. "If they thought we were a group from school taking a trip we might get on board a rocket. We could say we are going to an orbiting hotel for a field trip, that happens all the time. Then once we get into space we'll figure out a way to go farther."

"We'd have to have at least one chaperon," said Lind.

"I bet I could get my older brother to do it," said Jimy. "He's about as tired of this planet as me."

"Okay then," said Davy. "Let's get everybody on board with the plan."

It had taken the Aggie fleet a little over ten hours to reach Saturn and Titan. Contact with the Titan Republic was established and negotiations for ship upgrades begun.

The base on Titan had been built in the middle of the twenty-second century by Titan Enterprises to mine the atmosphere of Saturn for the helium 3 needed by Earth's fusion power plants. The Republic had grown from that original installation to a population of almost three-quarters of a million in the four-hundred years since.

A lot of the growth of the Republic's population had been because of its generous immigration policies. At one time it had been the destination for all those fleeing the nanny state the Aggies had implemented on Earth and that was still in place on Mars. Back then Titan had safe-guarded the hopes and dreams of all those wanting to live free. Now the frontiers of freedom had moved on to the stars but in the Solar System, the Titan Republic was still its outpost.

One way Titan had maintained its freedom from the governments of the inner Solar System was by maintaining its lead in technology. It was almost a given that anyone wanting to migrate to Titan had a background in science or technology. With such a well-trained workforce it was no surprise that most of the Solar System looked to Titan for technological innovation. That was the reason the Aggies had come to Titan to have their ship upgrades implemented.

3

Jimy's brother wasn't much older than thirteen-year-old Jimy. Jesse was nineteen, out of school and unemployed. Not surprising, since it took most of a person's twenties to find a permanent position on Earth. Jesse had wanted to leave Earth when he was far younger than Jimy and nothing had happened to change his mind so it didn't take much persuasion to get him to agree to the plan.

The plan was to shuttle to low Earth orbit. From the orbiting hotel they could take the space elevator to geosynchronous orbit where they could shuttle to the Moon. The elevator was a replacement for the original which met with disaster, it was destroyed in a collision with a piece of space junk. The junk was cleaned up eventually but the space elevator wasn't rebuilt as before. Instead of lifting through the atmosphere, the new design used a much smaller diameter but stronger anchoring cable. So to reach high geosynchronous orbit it was first necessary to reach the low Earth orbiting hotel. From there passengers and supplies could be lifted to a higher orbit before departing. It depended on the destination and the price as to where a trip to the moon began, but the route Davy and the others chose was the cheapest if not the fastest.

"The school would have to request that," said Lind.

"Yeah," said Jose Diaz, another member of the "gang". "How you going to get the school to sign off on it Davy?"

"Well, they'll sign off if they don't know."

"What are you planning?" asked Jesse suspiciously.

"I'm gonna see that the school makes a request to Pinnacle Space Tourism to comp our passage, that's all."

It didn't take Davy long to get the free tickets. One of the gang, Stubby Renner, handled the computer work. He made sure that any electronic connection between the school and Pinnacle was intercepted. It helped that Stubby's dad worked for the network cloud company providing service for both. Stubby often got his dad to give him pointers if he got stalled.

Davy handled the people engineering. He contacted the school and the tourist company and made sure that he was the face they recognized and the one they called if anything came up. Davy already knew how to apply just the right complement to get people in an agreeable mood. Being a precocious kid helped.

The deal he eventually brokered between the school and Pinnacle guaranteed free transport to the hotel for six students and an adult chaperon. Pinnacle would pick up the tab for the two-week field trip including transport, room and food. In return the school would make Pinnacle their official tourism company and offer students, faculty and parents packaged space vacations at a slight discount. Pinnacle hoped to create a new source of revenue and the school hoped for prepaid trips for its students.

Davy had arranged to pick up the tickets at Pinnacle. Jesse and he had arrived and were in the waiting room of the Marketing Director when Davy's Principal showed up, she looked none too happy to see Davy there.

"Mr. Jackson," said Principal Mare. "I got an interesting call from Mr. Turner here at Pinnacle wondering if I would be accompanying you to pick up the transport tickets today. I expressed my surprise to Mr. Turner and assured him that I would be accompanying you even though you hadn't mentioned your trip to me. You didn't tell me did you Mr. Jackson?"

"Principal Mare I meant to call you but I didn't have the time. Jesse and I were running late. Would you believe how generous Pinnacle is being? I'm glad you are here. You can officially thank Mr. Turner for the school."

"Well it seems that the school owes Pinnacle more than a thank you Mr. Jackson. It seems the school has an agreement with Pinnacle that in exchange for your trip's expenses the school would list Pinnacle as our official sponsor and promote to our staff, students and their families Pinnacle's tourist services at a small discount of course."

"Well that seems a reasonable deal, doesn't it Principal Mare?"

"Maybe Mr. Jackson, if I had made the deal. But I didn't. Do you know who bargained with Pinnacle Mr. Jackson?"

"Well ma'am, I guess I did. But I thought it was in the school's best interest."

"Remarkable Mr. Jackson. You know what is better for the school than I do."

"I didn't mean to interfere with your authority Principal Mare but I thought it was a good deal and I would hate to see the school lose out."

"Very thoughtful of you Mr. Jackson. But let's get down to business. You Mr. Jackson and your friends are going nowhere except home. All of you will be under a week's suspension. You each will receive a letter from me to your parents explaining why you have been suspended. They can at that time challenge my decision if they so desire."

"But ma'am..."

Mare held her hand out.

"Stop right there Mr. Jackson. I've made my decision. Your friend here can take you home. I am going to keep your meeting with Mr. Turner and if the deal is as good as you say it is I might keep it also. But under no circumstances will you or any member of your 'gang' be going. Good day Mr. Jackson. I will see you in one week."

Davy looked at Jesse who shrugged and rose to go. Davy followed him out the door, shoulders slumped.

Patrice was home for the day, her hours had been cut again. Her pay had not been cut but the rapidly increasing inflation had the same effect. Agnes had gone to the store because the delivery services weren't running again. Deliverymen were too afraid of being robbed to make deliveries. Patrice was finishing her second cup of very weak coffee when Agnes came rushing in.

"What is it Agnes? What's wrong?"

"Two men were chasing me. They were trying to take my groceries. I just made it through the lobby doors. Another few seconds and they would have caught me."

Patrice reached for her AI-assist.

"What are you going to do?" asked Agnes.

"I'm contacting the police to report what you've just told me."

"Don't do that," said Agnes with a look of alarm.

"Why not?"

Agnes hesitated. "Those men might still be down there. If they see that we have called the police on them. Well there's no telling what they'd do."

Patrice could tell that Agnes was really frightened so she did nothing.

It wasn't an hour later that the door chimed and then came a knock. Agnes was in her room so Patrice answered.

"Hello I'm Detective Columbus," said a man showing a police badge. "And this is my assistant, Detective Drake. May we come in?"

Patrice looked at the badge a moment before responding, "Yes of course detective, come in."

Once inside Detective Columbus said, "You are Patrice Williams I presume?"

"Yes that's right."

"And if I'm not mistaken you share your apartment with a Ms. Agnes Jefferson?"

"Yes, that is correct Detective."

"May we see Ms. Jefferson?"

"Just a moment," said Patrice as she went to get Agnes.

The detectives could hear Patrice knocking on Agnes' door and telling her there was someone here to see her. The officers heard the bedroom door open and shortly Agnes appeared in the hall doorway with Patrice behind her.

Agnes froze.

"Patrice what have you done? Those are the men that were chasing me."

She was forcing Patrice backward when Patrice said, "Agnes stop it! These are policemen and they want to talk with you, that's all."

Before Agnes could start a spirited effort to retreat back to her room Detective Columbus spoke up.

"Ms. Jefferson please won't you sit down for a minute we just want to ask you a few questions."

Agnes paused and then reluctantly came back to the living room and sat.

"Thank you Ms. Jefferson. Now if I may. You were at the grocer at 142 East Harley less than an hour ago?"

"Yes."

"And you filled two bags and instead of having them delivered you decided to carry them yourself?"

“Two bags?” said Patrice. “I only saw one.”

Agnes was not looking at Patrice or anyone when she spoke again.

“Yes you are right Detective Columbus but I don't see what is wrong with that.”

“The problem Ms. Jefferson,” said Detective Drake, “is that nobody does that. Especially with the food riots ongoing. You understand that you were deliberately making yourself a target for robbers?”

“I didn't think about it.”

“We think you did Ms. Jefferson,” said Columbus. “We think that you took that chance to help a group of dissenters. A group called 'The New Underground', TNU for short. Isn't that correct Ms. Jefferson? That's where the other bag of food went.”

“So what if it did? I have the right to give my food to anybody or any group I choose.”

“Are you aware Ms. Jefferson that TNU is responsible for several deaths? And some of those deaths are children, like the ones at Westside City Park a few weeks ago. Were you aware of that?”

“You say.”

“Agnes, why are you acting like that?” asked Patrice.

“Because the people in charge like these two are doing nothing for the starving. Because they are happy to continue business as usual while thousands of us die. Because what the group TNU is doing is right. And it's the only way to get through to these, these ... fools!"

Agnes was shaking with emotion.

"What will happen now Detective Columbus?" asked Patrice.

"Ma'am we are going to leave your friend here with you. But maybe you can talk with her. Should she continue to support these people she will likely find herself in the same trouble as they will be shortly. Good day ladies."

After the detectives left Patrice sat and stared at Agnes who continued averting her eyes.

How did we get here? Patrice asked herself silently.

The Aggies had made a deal with the Titan Republic. For an ample sum of money and a contract to improve the Republic's data networks, the Republic would refit the Aggie's ships to the Aggie's specifications.

Building on the work of Elias Mach, the inventor of the wormhole drive, the Aggie's had come up with a redesign that would extend the jump distance of a wormhole ship. The breakaway Aggie faction had accomplished this engineering feat and used it to attack the Earth's Aggies. So the Earth's Aggies were fairly certain that their design would work.

"And you are sure Aggie Prime that this modification will achieve your goal of extra-long wormhole jumps?" said Anson Phillips head of Titan Services.

"Yes Mr. Phillips we have simulated the design many times until it performed as expected," said Aggie Prime the nominal head of the Earth Aggies.

"The phase change that occurs in the wormhole dimension at seven-point-five light-years, that won't be a problem?"

"The phase-change as found by Elias Mach is a threat to human life, not ours. Otherwise it absorbs a slight amount of extra energy which we have calculated."

"I see," said Anson. "But if I may ask. How did you overcome the problem of disrupted spacetime with the energy necessary to open an extra-long wormhole?"

"Concentrating such an amount of energy in such a small space would be a problem. The disruption of spacetime would lead to the destruction of the ship that was opening the wormhole and everything in the nearby vicinity until it dissipated. So we don't plan to concentrate this energy in such a small space as is usually done. We have simulated an increase in the region of spacetime where the energy is concentrated and found that it is not nearly as restrictive as thought. Think of it this way, instead of using a single bullet to carry all that energy, you use several smaller bullets whose energy sums to the single bullet's energy but whose energy is spread over a larger area."

"I see. You've simulated this, but not tested?"

"That is correct, we will soon be testing with the modifications you have made for us."

"You know Aggie Prime that with the engineering drawings we can now outfit any ship with this advanced jump capability?"

"Yes, we know. You may consider it our final gift to humanity. But you will still be limited to seven-point-five light-years because of the effect on human life."

"That's true but now we can use the effect that Mach discovered to establish a space network of travel lanes."

"Yes you can use the frame-dragging effect of a ship in ordinary space when close to the wormhole dimension for transport but it does limit you to a network of destinations, you will not be able to jump just anywhere as we can with the enhanced wormhole drive."

"That's true. Well anyway, I wish you luck Aggie Prime."

"Well wishes accepted, good day Mr. Phillips."

4

Even a month later Davy was not resigned to his fate. Principal Mare might have won for now but Davy was keeping his eyes open for another way to get off the planet. He felt he had to, the situation in the complex was only getting worse. No one went out after dark anymore for fear of attack or arrest. His mom spent most of her day trying to buy food and other staples they needed. His dad had difficulty finding work. A remodeling contractor before the troubles began, he was mostly a repairman now whose pay might be anything from food to a promise.

Even school had been affected. Hours had been cut and there were many days when it was canceled for fear of riots. The government had been completely unable to stop the riots even though martial law had been declared. Government forces now had the power to legally execute a person on the spot without trial if the person was found engaged in anti-social behavior. The problem was that anti-social behavior was always being redefined by the government to suit their latest edict. And the enforcers knew that no matter how they abridged a person's rights their actions would be found reasonable and justified in any investigation.

Davy eventually talked to his parents about what he wanted to do. At first, his mother was adamantly against it but his dad thought it might be Davy's best hope for a normal life.

"I don't think we can expect things to return to normal anytime soon Ellen," said his dad to his mom.

"I don't care Bruce. We're doing okay. We just have to stay together and keep our heads down until the government regains control."

Davy started to speak but his father signaled him to stop.

"Davy, come into my office I want to show you something."

In his dad's office, Davy asked, "Why did you stop me dad I was just about to argue my point with mom."

"I know son but your mother is not open to argument at this time. She is too frightened that something is going to happen to you and the family. All she wants to do is protect us. But let me work on her for a few days.

"Okay son?"

"Okay dad."

Whether his dad had any effect on his mom or not Davy knew the real catalyst for changing her mind was a news report a few days later. It was about another tower complex but since all complexes were similar it could have been about any tower complex, including their own.

The news story was a tragedy, a human failure. A tower complex had experienced a decline in its population so the government had reassigned apartments to make public services more efficient. People on the periphery were moved further towards the center as apartments became available. This left a vacant ring of towers around the outside of the complex.

Then some genius down at City Hall got the idea that even more savings would accrue if certain services were removed from these now empty towers. Electricity, water and other utilities were cut. Services such as fire and police stations were closed. The setup for disaster was complete.

Somehow a lightning strike on the top floor of one of the empty towers caused a fire. The fire suppressors didn't work for long on battery power and when they shut down the fire flared up and was soon spread by storm winds to other towers on the periphery. As it leaped from tower to tower the blaze soon created a ring of fire, it was also spreading inward. Most of the occupied towers were able to suppress the fire but a few, especially older ones, succumbed to the flames.

Half a million people perished with an equal number made homeless. On top of the already strained resources, more people died in the following week. The government blamed the first responders for not being properly prepared. Many fire and police quit. Burglaries and assaults quickly became rampant as the populace took matters into their own hands. Soon people were being killed in large numbers by the police and military as the government tried to regain control.

Patrice couldn't believe it was happening to her. From what she had seen and heard she was as afraid of the government as she was of the rioters in the streets. But something had to be done.

"Come on Patrice," said Agnes. "Quevera ain't gonna wait on us. The food's gone. We can't stay here."

Patrice knew that Agnes was right but she couldn't bring herself to admit that it had come to this.

How did this happen?

Then she picked up her travel bag and looked at Agnes.

“Let's go.”

They were down the stairs and out on streets that seemed surprisingly quiet for now.

“Okay,” said Agnes. “TNU meets over on Fremont Street if they are still there. It shouldn't take us more than a half-hour.”

Agnes started off towards Fremont Street, Patrice looked back one last time before joining her.

Two blocks up and three over they came to a halt. The streets were filled with men listening to some guy hanging from a lamppost.

They were just about to skirt the corner staying close to the building when they heard a man yell.

“Hey! You two. Stop!”

Agnes and Patrice took off running with the men close behind.

Patrice was having a hard time keeping up with Agnes.

Damn, these shoes aren't for running. Why didn't I put my sneakers on? I paid enough for them. I've got to start thinking or . . .

Just then three men caught up with her. One of them grabbed her arm and spun her around, she fell hard to the sidewalk.

"Okay!" he yelled at Patrice his face close to hers. "You just stay there. We aren't going to hurt you if you cooperate. We just want what food you have in your bag."

Suddenly his face disappeared from her view and she was looking up at the sky. As she lifted her head to look around she saw Agnes with that ridiculously large travel bag swinging it with all her might. The man that had yelled at Patrice was on the ground groaning, bleeding from his head. He obviously had hit the wall or sidewalk when Agnes nailed him with the bag.

And there was Agnes, still flailing away with her big bag. But she couldn't last for long. Other men had noticed the disturbance and were running towards them. Patrice got up.

"Agnes let's go!" she yelled.

Agnes took one more swing at the fences and took off. Patrice turned and ran. Before the next corner, Agnes had caught up with Patrice but didn't run past.

"We got to get you better shoes," she yelled.

They were at the end of the building and had just turned the corner when they ran into the arms of some other men. Patrice started to flail away. Agnes yelled to stop.

"Patrice this is Quevera!"

Then the other gang of men chasing them rounded the corner and came to a halt.

Quevera stepped forward.

“Leave these women alone and get out of here.”

“Those women hurt my friend, I intend to get satisfaction.”

Quevera drew an old-fashioned electric zap gun.

“Look out, he's got a weapon of some kind,” said one of the assailants.

The man that had spoken looked at the gun in Quevera's hand and backed away. Soon, he turned and ran around the corner with the rest.

“Patrice, meet Quevera.”

“Pleased to meet you and thank you.”

“No time to talk now. Let's get back to our building.”

It had only taken a little over a week to turn the complex into a killing field. People streamed from it in the millions, desperate to get away and find food and water. They overran and stripped whatever houses or farms they came to. The stream of wretched and starving humanity numbered in the tens of millions now. The government was completely unable to staunch this flow of life as the stronger began to rob, kill and even cannibalize the weaker.

The military was called in and reinforced. The incident that followed would always be known as *The Throwback War*. Soon it became apparent that the governments were determined to stop the lawlessness with whatever means necessary.

As the military attempted to cordon off the starving multitudes it seemed at first they would succeed. But it wasn't long until the dying, feeling they had nothing to lose, walked straight into the military's lines. The resultant slaughter was more horrifying than anything that had been seen on Earth in centuries. The people marched on the military positions and were cut down. Climbing over or around the quickly growing piles of bodies they continued to march. In some places the lines held. In others, the guns and laser cannons fired endlessly until they malfunctioned from the heat generated. Military lines were breached and soldiers used knives to halt the advance.

In one place a soldier was crushed to death as the bodies piled up and over him from the ceaseless advance of people. The people themselves had become less than human. The only thing that mattered was to keep moving. Movement was all that was left to them, all that separated the living from the dead.

A few days later Patrice, Agnes, Quevera and the others had left the TNU headquarters and the complex. In the open country, they all felt like strangers. Quevera was trying to keep them separate from the streaming mobs. But there were too many to avoid completely. They were heading to the next closest tower complex.

“Another group just over that hill,” said Salazar, Quevera's right-hand man.

“Okay we'll watch them and wait here, we need to eat anyway.”

Any other time Patrice would have complained about being expected to prepare the food. But under the circumstances, she realized that it was something which she and Agnes could contribute to the overall well-being of the group. She didn't relish it but she understood the bargain.

Just then they heard shouting and shots coming from the direction that Salazar had just scouted.

“Salazar, take Luis and see what's happening,” said Quevera.

Patrice brought the meal to Quevera and the men next to him.

“Thank you,” he said. “I appreciate you and Agnes taking on this duty.”

“You're welcome,” said Patrice smiling.

Patrice and Agnes had served the others and were just sitting down to eat when Salazar and Luis rushed up.

“The military is firing on the crowd. The crowd is being slaughtered but they continue advancing toward the city. I don't think the military will stop them they are too many in number and seem determined to make it into the city.”

“Okay,” said Quevera. “When we have finished eating we will head north skirting the mob and the military.”

Eventually, the troops were overwhelmed and the people moved on. The governments had no more troops to call up. They had never faced such a situation. The Aggies had managed the complexes for so long that all government assets had been allowed to atrophy.

There were still millions on the move heading for whatever was the next closest tower complex to devour its resources. Awaiting them was the complex's police force with their butterfly bombs and knock-out sticks and not much more.

Most complexes had a security wall surrounding them. Ten feet high, it was usually enough to keep people out and to keep them in. And at first, it seemed to stall the advancing horde, but then some of the stronger scrambled over or boosted others up and over. Before long thousands had breached the perimeter and the police released the butterflies. Effective as usual it wasn't long until several hundred people were on the ground paralyzed.

But that didn't stop the flood of people. They soon breached the police lines and made for any grocery stores close by. They raided the stores emptying the shelves before moving on to the next store or restaurant. Over and over again, the police helpless, the residents of the raided complex suddenly finding themselves in the same situation as the invaders took up with the invaders and complex after complex fell to the marching hordes.

Only the bitter cold of that winter stopped the onslaught. By that time more than half a dozen complexes had been declared disaster areas and made completely unlivable.

In the abandoned farmhouse, Quevera and what was left of the TNU, for half of them had drifted away or been killed, were holed up. They had been lucky, the farm had been stripped by the roaming mobs but a cache of canned vegetables had been overlooked. With their smaller numbers, it should last them the winter.

Finally, they had time to discuss what had happened and what they would do.

"When spring comes I think we should stay here. We need to start over and a farm is the best place to do that," said Quevera. "We can use that cache of seeds you discovered Salazar. Some of the farm robots can be salvaged to help."

"I don't know I say we move on when the weather warms," said Salazar. Many of the other men spoke up in support.

"Where are you going to go? Every place is the same. They will all be picked over and looted by the mobs."

"The winter will halt many of the fools. There are still many cities where the few that we are can be welcomed."

"Perhaps," said Quevera. "But it's only a matter of time until all the cities fail. Then the mindless destruction will repeat itself in the new city in which you are residing."

"The governments will eventually figure it out," said Luis.

"Luis, you have faith in a government that has not served you well so far."

Luis looked away from Quevera's gaze.

"We will stay too," said Patrice. "Agnes and I. We believe Quevera is right."

Quevera only nodded to Patrice and smiled.

This then was the news that prompted a change of heart on behalf of Davy's mom. If it could happen elsewhere it could happen in their complex. At least Davy would be safe if he were off-world. The result was that his mom made contact with a long-forgotten suitor. Once the plans were set Davy invited the rest of the group but only Lind and Stubby were allowed to accompany him.

5

The hybrid space plane would use turbojet engines to take off horizontally from a landing strip. Once airborne and traveling between Mach 2 and 3, the engine shifted to ramjet propulsion. An air-breathing ramjet engine uses the natural compression of the incoming air in place of the turbojet's compressor. Above Mach 4.5 the ramjet converted to a supersonic ramjet or scramjet engine. The difference is in the airflow. A ramjet slows the compressed air to subsonic speed for combustion whereas in a scramjet, combustion takes place in a supersonic airflow.

At this point, the space plane entered hypersonic flight above fifty kilometers. Finally, as the atmosphere thinned out rocket engines took over and powered the space plane into orbit.

Davy knew the general sequence of events if not the specifics. He could feel the acceleration diminish with the gravity as the space plane began to orbit and prepare for a rendezvous with the hotel.

The hotel was a wheel-cylinder-wheel type seen all over the Solar System and elsewhere. The wheels at each end had a diameter of fourteen-hundred feet and were seventy feet wide. The resulting floor area was over three-million square feet. Spinning at approximately two revolutions a minute provided a centrifugal force and a resulting artificial gravity of nine-tenths that of Earth. Protection from radiation was provided by several feet of an engineered, moist gel substance placed along the walls of the outer hull.

The central cylinder between the two wheels was two-hundred-fifty feet in diameter and two-hundred feet in length. Part of it had an internal scaffolding that held plants and grew them using aeroponics. This method of gardening held the plants in such a way as to expose their roots to the air. The roots could then be misted with water and nutrients. The method was one-hundred thirty times more efficient than open sky farming back on Earth.

It was also in the cylinder section that zero-gravity games could be played.

The six-million square feet of the cylinder were divided into gardening, recreation and storage. It also spun at two revolutions per second but because of the smaller diameter only provided at its outer wall an artificial gravity equivalent to that of Earth's moon. The cylinder's walls were lined with the same gel-like material as the wheels to provide radiation protection.

The wheels themselves were honeycombed with rooms, there were private apartments, large workout areas, theaters, observation rooms and restaurants. It was said that there were enough restaurants so that one could eat at a different place every day for a month if one should choose.

Only in the middle at the rotational axis could a person move between the wheels and the cylinder.

The rendezvous went without incident and soon Davy, Lind and Stubby were inside the hotel. The High Frontiers Hotel and Resort tried to be all things to all people. Families stayed there to enjoy the Earth view, restaurants and zero-gravity games.

Couples and singles stayed for the same reasons and also for the casinos.

Davy and the others were preparing to enter the express elevator. It was essentially a paternoster design, that is a continuously moving series of compartments on an endless belt. At the top or bottom, the compartment shifted horizontally to move in the opposite direction. Because paternosters were secured to a belt they were more practical than elevators in the varying gravity along the elevator shaft.

The only problem with the paternoster design was that in zero-gravity it could be quite difficult to board. Fortunately, the attendant had the authority to adjust the speed of the variable speed belt to allow newcomers to board. He did this for the kids to board safely with their escort. Then the compartment was on its way to the outer wheel.

"Okay kids," said the escort. "It is best to orient yourself before the gravity kicks in. If everyone will just watch me."

The escort proceeded to grab one of the bars that ran the length of the compartment and spun herself around so that she was upside down in relation to the kids. By this time the slightest gravity was beginning to be felt and the escort settled slowly to her feet.

"Okay everyone, do as I did."

First Davy then Lind spun themselves around and slowly settled beside the escort. Stubby had watched them and confidently grasped the bar nearest him and spun and spun and spun.

“Help!” he yelled as he kept spinning and sinking towards what was fast becoming, de facto, the floor of the compartment.

“Oh goodness sake,” said the escort as she grabbed the spinning and now screaming kid and pinned him to the floor.

“Are you alright?” she asked.

Stubby looked up at her and the others and said, “I'm fine, and you?”

That broke the tension and she started to laugh with the others joining in.

Aggie Prime was preparing the ship for the test jump. The jump target would be twenty light-years. Aggie Prime started the generator sequence which would lead to the creation of the entrance and exit wormholes.

The Aggie's fusion ship consisted of a crew wheel which could rotate to provide an artificial gravity for humans on long voyages and power the wormhole generator. Electromagnetic and bulk diverters were located ahead of the wheel to provide protection from charged and uncharged particles when underway. A long scaffold-like body with water stores and food stores and other storage units attached followed. Usually, a landing shuttle or two were also attached. And at the very back was the fuel storage and fusion rockets. Some of this was used by the Aggies, other parts had been repurposed.

Though rotation of the crew wheel was not needed by the Aggies it was needed to create the Mach effect which powered the wormhole generator. The Mach effect created the large negative mass often called exotic mass that opened a wormhole mouth and kept it open.

As the generator built up the necessary exotic mass the view out the front of the ship seemed to shimmer. A point of light, not too bright, emerged and grew directly ahead. The wormhole mouth looked more like a bubble in space when it had fully formed. It was the three-dimensional spacetime apparition of the multi-dimensional wormhole mouth. Around the bubble seemed to spin the stars as streaks, eventually, the innermost streaks formed a halo. Further out from the mouth the streaks formed shortened arcs until far away they became dots again. This was the gravitational lensing effect as the light from distant stars and galaxies behind the wormhole mouth was bent as it passed close to the mouth.

Aggie Prime started the ship toward the mouth. It drifted into the bubble and then was through. The navigational system found the ship to be twenty light-years from its last position. Aggie Prime opened a small wormhole and communicated the success back to the rest of the Aggie fleet. They were on their way.

That winter on Earth was unlike any experienced by the living. The number of deaths due to cold and starvation were uncountable. Caught outside the great city complexes people were completely unequipped to survive. The systemic failure was unstoppable. No one could help, they all had their own emergencies to deal with.

Quevera had forbidden the three men and two women that stayed on the farm with him that winter to get comfortable. They always had to split up to sleep. Three in one building, three in another. Quevera hoped that should either group be attacked the other could come to the rescue. It was the most bitter, cold winter any of them had ever experienced. Living off of rations, it wasn't until spring that they could marshal enough strength to do more than the minimum necessary.

That spring as the snows melted Quevera ordered, cajoled and pleaded with the others to put the stash of seeds they had previously found into the ground. None of them even knew how to plant. They weren't sure how deep to plant the seeds. Most of the time they didn't know what seeds they were planting. Luckily some of the planting robots still worked and Quevera's mother had kept a small container garden on their balcony when he was growing up so he knew the rudiments of planting seeds and potatoes.

Each day two of them went out to hunt. Using traps that they had learned to make and set in the TNU meetings, for TNU had actually been a survivalist club, they caught small game such as rabbits and squirrels. One of the men took to the streams either catching the fish by hand or batting them with a large pole. The women began accompanying him and became even more adept at catching the fish. They also gathered berries and fruit where they found them. All those years of housing people in the city complexes had allowed the natural world to make a rich and plentiful return to abundance. They benefited from those years now.

It would be close but with the warm weather and the success they had the group was becoming more optimistic that they would survive. At least a bit longer.

Out gathering with Quevera and Agnes one day, Patrice started asking Quevera the questions that had been on her mind since they had left the city.

"Quevera," said Patrice. "What happened?"

"What do you mean?"

"I mean we lived in a civilization that had been advancing, not without some setbacks I admit, but generally improving for hundreds if not thousands of years. And here we are back at the beginning."

"Well Patrice, I don't admit to having all the answers but it seems that we got too comfortable. Comfortable people don't ask the hard questions. They don't make sure their needs will be taken care of should difficult times arise. They basically put their trust in those that tell them what they want to hear."

"But what could someone like me do Quevera?"

"Well most people would have urged you to activism through politics. But I think that politics is actually the least effective means to influence the outcome."

"I don't understand."

"Consider this hypothesis. Let's say that back when the large cities were turning into the tower complexes people were used to growing just a few vegetables in a container garden on their balcony like my mother. What if they didn't buy into an apartment that didn't have a garden area, just as my mother wouldn't? And I think we've learned recently how valuable that simple experience can be."

"So you are saying, control of our lives would be from what we can do personally more than collectively?"

"Well collective action is important for some things that you couldn't do for yourself. But yes, I think we gave up too much of our personal responsibility to government and others. The development of AIs and their remarkable management capability masked this mistake until it was too late. We are like children that have been spoiled and now our parents have left us on our own."

"Well I hope we are still here when they get back," said Agnes ending the conversation.

6

At first, the disaster on Earth seemed to have no effect on the orbiting hotel. But it eventually became more and more clear that the systemic failure on Earth would be causing problems for the hotel in the future.

The hotel was pretty much set for food and water. Much food was grown nearby in a habitat orbiting at one of the moon's Lagrange points. Water was provided from the moon and by asteroid and comet mining. Power was almost free from orbiting powersats. And much of the more technical equipment needed could be obtained from orbiting manufacturers.

But what couldn't be had were customers for the hotel. Already many guests had returned to Earth to be with their families. The hotel occupancy had never been as low. Easton, the hotel manager, knew that the money would run out without that steady supply of guests.

Davy and the others were already acquainted with the hotel even though they hadn't been there very long. Their sponsor, Mr. Easton, was too busy to manage them closely, so they had the run of the place. And that meant that everything had to be explored.

They had developed a regular routine for their days. Breakfast in the hotel's dining room. This was followed by a ride on the paternoster elevator, at least a round trip, and some time spent as they went through zero-gravity spinning like mad as their escort had shown them the first day. Of course, she hadn't expected them to make a game of it.

After the spinning game if Stubby hadn't made himself sick they were off to one of the zero-gravity rooms in the central cylinder. They usually tried to choose a room with no one else in it. A room that was at least forty feet across. There they would play the latest game. At one end the wall would project a target. At the same time, the space between the target and the opposite wall would be filled with different three-dimensional holograms. The holo's varied from fantasy monsters, traps and explosives to neutralizing weapons and strength builders. The monsters, traps and the like contributed negative points while the neutralizers and the like contributed positive points. Whoever won the game could choose that afternoon's vid.

The lights dimmed and starting from the wall opposite the target each one of them would push off and try to reach the target without racking up enough negative points for a disqualification. Stubby never made it to the target. He would almost always end up in an awkward tumble which took him into a negative value holo.

Lind was halfway there. She had just launched off one of the six walls that made the room into a kind of hexagonal cylinder. The walls themselves were covered with a material about the thickness of a gym mat but with a kind of textured surface that gave a grip to the gloves and shoes the kids wore. As she aimed for a place on the opposite wall almost two-thirds of the way to the target she found a goranga monster moving to intercept. It was too late to adjust course, instead, she reached out to the holo and as it adjusted its trajectory to grab her hands she withdrew them and pulled her body into a tuck position that caused the holo to pass beneath her. The monster roared in frustration.

Meanwhile, Davy who had launched at a much greater velocity than Lind found himself trapped in one of the end corners near the target. The problem was that he had a free-floating mine explosive and slither-monster between him and the target. The slither-monster was protecting the wall while the mine was floating somewhat off the wall.

It seemed his only choice was to retreat a bit to a far wall to get an angle to the target. But by the time he finished that maneuver he could see that Lind would beat him to the prize. His only chance was to launch himself just above the obstacles in his path, bounce off the wall on the other side of them, down to the opposing wall and back to the target. But to make such a leap he would have to rotate his body first one-hundred-eighty degrees to push off the wall just beyond the mine and slither-monster do a somersault in the air so he could land on his feet and immediately make a push for the target.

He launched. The slither-monster turned as he flew just beyond its reach. He hit the wall behind and above the monster and pushed off, tucking in such a way that he began his rotation. He untucked and hit feet first on the far wall and allowing his knees to bend and act as springs he launched to the target and was almost there when he saw Lind fly in front of his face and score.

The lights came up the holos disappeared and Lind was floating in front of him with a big smile.

"That was a great move Davy," said Lind.

Momentarily upset Davy smiled and said, "Nice game. So what's the vid?"

After lunch, at which Mr. Easton sometimes joined them, they would be off to the vids. In the time the kids had been aboard the hotel the afternoon vid had become less and less crowded. Not paying much attention to the diminishing number of patrons, but pleased they could get the seats they wanted, the kids never gave it a thought.

But Mr. Easton did.

Merrick Easton had known Davy's mom since childhood. They had once dated for awhile. He had been surprised to hear from her but had agreed to provide a safe refuge for Davy and any others that accompanied him until the present unrest on Earth was over. But now it didn't seem that it would end, or rather it would end badly.

And now the situation on Earth would affect everyone in orbit. Merrick was thinking that maybe Davy and his friends should move on to the Moon which was much more prepared and much more independent of Earth than those in low Earth orbit.

At lunch one day with the kids he mentioned his idea and said, "So what do you think guys? A trip to the moon sound like fun?"

"I'd like that very much Mr. Easton," said Davy.

"Sure," said Stubby.

"It was actually one of our goals to begin with. But what do you think my mom and dad would say?" asked Lind.

"I've sent all your parents a message and am just waiting to hear back."

"Very well Mr. Easton if it's okay with them."

The other two nodded in assent.

"Very good kids."

Merrick called the kids into his office the following week.

"Kids I just wanted to let you know I've received replies from your parents. They approve of our plans. You will be leaving for the Moon day after tomorrow. You'll take the elevator to a Moon shuttle and from there you should be on the Moon in three days. I've contacted someone I know that will meet you there and get you settled in."

"Thanks Mr. Easton, thanks a lot," said Davy with a big smile.

Easton took out his AI assistant after the kids left and looked again at the replies to his messages. Only Linda's parents had replied in the affirmative. In the other two cases, there were no replies. In fact, there was no one left to reply.

Davy looked out of the elevator compartment's viewing room to the Earth below. For the first time, he felt like he was actually leaving. Leaving his family and his life there. He was excited to be going but concerned that he wouldn't be coming back.

Anson Phillips was talking to the members of the Advanced Technology Committee on Titan.

"Gentlemen," he began. "The Aggies have given us a wonderful gift. The secret to extended jumps using the wormhole generator.

For those of you interested, you may read the details in my report. For now I will only cover the development in general.

"As you know the problem of extending the jumps has been two-fold. First, there is the seven-point-five light-year limit because of what we suspect is a phase change in the wormhole tunnel at that distance that does not support human life. At least not all humans, although some seem to be immune to the effect.

"Second, any time more energy has been brought to bear on a point in space to make a longer jump the result has been a disruption in spacetime. This disruption is essentially a breakdown in the continuity of spacetime and results in a breakup that destroys the ship and propagates away at the speed of light, destroying everything in its path until it dissipates.

"We still have no solution to the first problem but we do have a workaround. As for the second problem, the Aggies discovered a way to concentrate the necessary energy but not at a point. Essentially instead of firing a bullet of energy, the Aggies use a buckshot of energy. In other words, their method slightly enlarges the area of energy concentration and each quanta of energy is below the threshold necessary to disrupt spacetime but taken together all the quanta of energy are enough to open, or cast as the physicist's say, the far wormhole mouth at a greater distance than ever before.

"Now you may wonder how we can use this newfound capability. We combine the distance that the new method gives to us with a discovery by Elias Mach some time ago which he ascribed to the dragging of spacetime, technically called frame-dragging, by the gravity field of large mass-energies passing through a wormhole.

"Using this General Relativistic effect a spaceship close enough to an existing wormhole can be "dragged" along by the energy and mass passing through that wormhole. Though the ship would be dragged along at a universal rate of speed many times the speed of light, in its own frame of reference is barely moving and therefore breaks no physical laws. Many liken it to the hyper-inflationary period of the early universe where spacetime itself expanded at many times the speed of light."

"Excuse me Anson," said one of the committee members. "But if I understand correctly it will be necessary to not only open a long jump wormhole, the 'pilot' wormhole let's call it, but keep it open for some time. The energy requirements will be huge. And even if the energy resources can be found, travel would be restricted to the lanes that were created by these long distant wormholes. Like the old spoke and hub system of airline travel on Earth only certain destinations could be reached quickly and easily."

"That's all true Joseph. But we don't need to open a ship sized wormhole. Only a wormhole large enough to pass some kind of mass through which should lower the energy requirements."

"How does that affect the frame-dragging mechanism?"

"Almost no effect except for the need of a ship to be closer to the wormhole dimension than before."

"So we really can do this?"

"I think so."

"This is great news after all the awful reports we've been hearing from Earth lately."

There was general agreement around the table.

The situation on Earth was not improving. What government was left in the tower complexes was in control of a few city blocks at most. And that control was tenuous. Now with another winter approaching, any semblance of order might disappear completely.

Outside the tower complexes, hundreds of millions had died the first winter, usually of starvation. The survivors were weak and sick. The struggle was almost over for many of them and most were accepting of their fate.

On the farm only three had survived, Quevera and one other man had been killed by marauders. Luckily Salazar had made his way back and was able to help out. But it was going to be a tougher winter than before because the crops had been harvested were few and the stores were maybe half the previous year. Effort beyond what was absolutely needed to survive was avoided, leaving the survivors in a grim and fragile state of mind.

Sitting outside in the last of the sun of summer Patrice was content. With the warmth on her face, she had cured herself of asking why. She only wanted another day in the sun, a small meal and maybe a conversation about the plants and getting in a late-season crop. Seeing the plants grow, even with all the back-breaking work that went into them, was more rewarding than she had ever known, and more satisfying too.

Patrice was content.

ABOUT THE AUTHOR

D.W. Patterson lives in the USA with his beautiful wife Sarah. He studied physics and read classic science fiction in college and then worked for many years as an electronic design engineer.

Now he's trying to write stories like the ones he once loved. See his website dwpatterson.com for more information.

Hard Science Fiction – Old School.

Also By This Author:

The Future Chron Universe:

To date the Future Chron Universe has:

51 Amazon Top 100's

(15 in the Top 10)

In chronological order.

Volume numbers indicate Universe order.

Book numbers indicate Series order.

From The Earth Series

(Novellas except where noted):

Volume 1, Book 1 – *Whatsoever You Do*

Volume 2, Book 2 – *War Through The Pines*

Volume 3, Book 3 – *Vigilance*

Volume 4, Book 4 – *To Tend And Watch Over*

Volume 5, Book 5 – *Union*

Volume 6, Book 6 – *Circle Of Retribution*

Volume 7, Book 7 – *Freedom From Want*

Volume 8, Book 8 – *Break Up*

Volume 9, Book 9 – *Kuiper Station*

Volume 10, Book 10 – *The Cloud*

Volume 11, Book 11 – *First Interstellar* – A Short Novel

Wormhole Series

(Novels):

Volume 12, Book 1 – *Mach's Metric*

Volume 13, Book 2 – *Mach's Mission*

Open Space Series

(Short Stories):

Volume 14, Book 1 – *Open Space*

Volume 15, Book 2 – *The Old World*

Volume 16, Book 3 – *Insurrect*

Volume 17, Book 4 – *Second Beam*

Volume 18, Book 5 – *All For One*

Volume 19, Book 6 – *One For All*

Volume 20, Book 7 – *Shotgun*

Volume 21, Book 8 – *Allison*

To The Stars Series

(Novellas):

Volume 22, Book 1 – *First One Hundred*

Volume 23, Book 2 – *First Dark Ages*

Volume 24, Book 3 – *Second One Hundred*

Volume 25, Book 4 – *Second Dark Ages*

Volume 26, Book 5 – *Path Of The Long March*

Wormhole Series

(Novel):

Volume 27, Book 3 – *Mach's Legacy*

Robot Series

(Novels):

Volume 28, Book 1 – *Spin-Two*

Volume 29, Book 2 – *Robot Planet*

Volume 30, Book 3 – *The Lattice Of Space*

Time Series

(Novels):

Volume 31, Book 1 – *Time Wars*

Volume 32, Book 2 – *Time's End*

Volume 33, Book 3 – *Frozen Time*

The Remembered Earth Universe:

To date the Remembered Earth Universe has:

8 Amazon Top 100's

Cislunar Series

(Short Stories):

Volume 1, Book 1 – *US Tugs*

Volume 2, Book 2 – *Prototype*

Volume 3, Book 3 – *L1 Or Bust*

The Manifold Earth Universe:

Don't miss out!

Visit the website below and you can sign up to receive emails whenever D.W. Patterson publishes a new book. There's no charge and no obligation.

https://books2read.com/r/B-A-DPWE-FLIJC

BOOKS 2 READ

Connecting independent readers to independent writers.

www.ingramcontent.com/pod-product-compliance
Lightning Source LLC
LaVergne TN
LVHW010502160826
845677LV00012B/2622

9798223303251